THE POWDER MONKEY

Young Americans Series #4

By
Carole R. Campbell

WHITE MANE KIDS

This White Mane Books publication
was printed by
Beidel Printing House, Inc.
63 West Burd Street
Shippensburg, PA 17257-0152 USA

In respect for the scholarship contained herein, the acid-free paper used in this book meets the guidelines for permanence and dura-
bility of the Committee on Production Guidelines for Book Longevity
of the Council on Library Resources.

For a complete list of available publications
please write
White Mane Books
Division of White Mane Publishing Company, Inc.
P.O. Box 152
Shippensburg, PA 17257-0152 USA

Library of Congress Cataloging-in-Publication Data

Campbell, Carole R., 1939-
    The powder monkey / by Carole R. Campbell.
        p.   cm. -- (Young Americans series : #4)
    Summary: In the second year of the Civil War, Tad Lynch becomes
trapped below deck on a Confederate warship and is pressed into
service during a two day battle between the Merrimack and three
Union ships.
    ISBN 1-57249-170-1 (alk. paper)
    [1. Merrimack (Frigate) Fiction. 2. United States--History--Civil
War, 1861–1865--Naval operations Fiction. 3. Hampton Roads (Va.),
Battle of, 1862 Fiction.] I. Title. II. Series.
PZ7.C15085Po   1999
[Fic]--dc21   99-21655
                                                                    CIP

PRINTED IN THE UNITED STATES OF AMERICA

Dedicated to my husband
R. Thomas Campbell—
Father, Author, Mentor, Friend

His research and knowledge
of the War Between the States
has made this book possible.

Contents

Illustrations

Characters

Tad Lynch[*]
Paul Lynch, Carpenter[*]
Mrs. Lynch, Mother[*]
Becky Lewis, Friend[*]
Jimmy Allen, Friend[*]
Shorty, Powder Boy[*]

Captain Franklin Buchanan
Lieutenant Catesby R. Jones
Lieutenant Charles C. Simms
Lieutenant John Taylor Wood
Lieutenant John R. Eggleston
Lieutenant Robert D. Minor
Surgeon D. B. Phillips
Chief Engineer Henry A. Ramsay
Gunner Charles B. Oliver

---

[*] Fictitious Characters

Gunner's Mate William Johnson
Master at Arms William H. Norris
Officer's Cook James Shever
Coal Heaver John W. Walton
Seaman Charles Wilson

1

The Hatch Was Closed!

"You poor skinny thing! Are you hungry, little fella? How did you get on this big ship? Do the sailors know that you are on board?" Tad asked as he stooped to pet the thin black cat.

"Mew!" cried the timid animal as it rubbed against the Tad's ankle again, seeming to know just what the boy was saying.

"Mind you, lad," Paul Lynch warned his son. "You have to be off the ship as soon as we finish the doors on the hatches," he shouted above all the noise from the carpenters' hammers.

"Yes, Pa," answered Tad as the frightened cat squeezed past his legs. Then it ran over to the next hatch and scampered to the deck below. Tad rushed to the opening to see if he could spot the animal. Not seeing it, he slowly eased himself down the ladder.

His eyes took a few minutes to adjust to the darkness below deck after being in the bright sunshine. "This must be the galley," he whispered to himself. There were large ovens with shiny doors. And built into the bulkhead was what looked like a giant icebox.

"Me-ow," came another plea for food, as the cat circled with its tail standing straight up.

"Let me see if I can find some cream in here for you, kitty." After looking to his right and then to his left, Tad carefully pulled at the large handle. Nothing. He pulled a bit harder, but it still didn't open. This time he yanked with all his might. The door flew open and several items came crashing out and onto the deck. Before he knew it, both he and the animal were standing in a puddle of cream. The kitten lapped up the cream as fast as his tongue could go in and out of his tiny mouth.

"Must find a rag. Got to clean up this mess before Pa discovers what I have done," Tad muttered to himself. Peering beyond the main part of the galley, his eyes fell upon some shelves and boxes. He moved quickly, for he knew he had little time. Just as he was going to reach into one of the boxes, a "Thud!" sounded.

"There may be another broom in here, mate."

"I told yuh to bring all the brooms topside," another voice scolded. "We're tuh sweep up all the wood shavings left from the carpenters." When he heard the word *brooms*, Tad quickly leaped into one of the large wooden crates, for there was a broom in the pantry right beside him.

As the two men argued, one reached for the broom next to the box where Tad was hiding. "Well I'll be d . . . Who made this mess in muh galley?" shouted the cook. "Look! It's that cat ag'in! Now someone's feed'n it. Mind yuh, that's the cream fer the Cap'n's tea. If I get my hands on that mate . . ."

Tad held his breath and tried not to move a single part of his body. The men sounded angry— even angrier than his mother was whenever he walked on the freshly scrubbed kitchen floor at home. He hadn't meant to spill the cream, and he really *was* looking for a rag to mop it up. Slowly letting the air out of his lungs, he quietly drew in another breath. His hands began to tremble. He couldn't see anything except the inside of the crate, but he could hear the men cursing and shoving things around. *Got to get back to Pa*, he thought. *I was to stay on board for only a short while.*

Suddenly, the bottom of the crate began to vibrate. Tad's whole body seemed to be quivering. *The engines!* The creaking and the groaning of the huge ship along with the rumble of the engines thundered in Tad's ears.

His mind raced. *Have to find Pa.* He shuddered to think that he might be too late. After the sailors had left and gone topside, Tad raced through the galley. It was 11:00 a.m. A signal gun boomed and bells rang. Tad clawed his way up the ladder, only to be met with a sudden "Wham!" Too late. The hatch was closed. Things went spinning before his eyes. Everything was a blur.

2

Everything Was Dark

"I think he's the son of one of the carpenters," said the brawny sailor.

"How did he get down here?" inquired another. "Now we're stuck with him. Old Buck is not going to like this."

Tad heard the voices of the sailors, yet they seemed far away—as though he were dreaming. Yet he could feel someone touching his forehead. He heard them say, "Old Buck." Yes, Tad had heard about Old Buck. Pa had told him that he must show respect for the commanding officer and call him "Captain Buchanan," even if the man did seem gruff. As he lay there, Tad's mind swirled with confused thoughts. *Ship's galley . . . need to get on deck . . .*

5

find Pa . . . get off before the Virginia *sails.* Suddenly
he felt himself being carried by strong arms.

"Got to hide the little twerp for now. It was my
job to see that all workmen and other civilians were
off the ship. I don't want double nightwatch,"
grumbled the sailor.

"Put him in a hammock back in the stern,"
ordered another. "Old Buck rarely inspects that part
of the ship."

"But Lieutenant Jones might!" responded the
other mate.

"Better Jones, than Buck. At least Jones is a bit
more forgiving. Let's get out of here. Out'n the
lantern."

* * * * *

Tad's head was throbbing. He felt his eyelids
and lashes. Yes, they seemed to be open, yet everything was dark. As he turned his head and his eyes
focused, he could see a slit of light along the floor,
or rather the *deck*, as his father had corrected him
earlier. He turned slightly and felt a swaying sen-
sation. He moved again . . . more swinging. He
finally realized that he was perched like a baby bird
in a swinging trap. He was cold and he was hungry,
and his head hurt. He missed his mother. Whenever
he was sick she would bring him chicken soup. If
he was cold when it was time to go to bed, she would

heat the iron on the wood stove, wrap it in a clean towel and put it at his feet, and then cover him with the quilt until he felt warm and cozy.

And he missed Scamp, the family's golden retriever. Every morning the shaggy dog came bounding into his room, licking Tad's nose until he sat up in bed to let the dog play tug-of-war with the blanket.

Tad had begged to be taken down to the docks, so that he could see the ship where Pa had been working. It had been the USS *Merrimack*, a warship that had been burned and scuttled at the navy yard by the Federals and then taken over by the Confederate Navy. He had heard people talking about how the War Between the States was a terrible thing . . . people fighting against each other in the same land! His father, Paul Lynch, supported the South and helped do his part by doing some volunteer work after hours. He had been one of the many who had helped raise the sunken *Merrimack*. Then the men cleared the splintered timbers from the top of the ship, worked to rebuild it, and added more powerful guns. The craft was renamed, and was now known as the CSS *Virginia*.

Just two days ago the crew had hauled hundreds of bags of gunpowder on board that would be used to fire the ten guns that were on the *Virginia*. Now after two days of wind and rain, March 8, 1862, showed blue skies and fluffy white clouds—just the weather for which Captain Buchanan was waiting. Now the huge ironclad could be taken for a trial run.

Tad had gone wide-eyed when he first saw the *Virginia* earlier in the day. He remembered saying to his father, "This thing looks like a giant wall of iron . . . just like the roof of a house floating on the water!"

Pa had explained how he and the other carpenters had hammered the wooden beams together so that the slanted part was about twenty-four inches thick. On top of that was attached four inches of iron, making an immense sloping casemate. All morning the sailors had been smearing grease over the casemate so that any enemy shells would glance off in the event that the ship was hit. The *Virginia* was moored in the shallow waters of the Elizabeth River which flows into Hampton Roads. At first Tad thought that "the Roads" were streets that crossed each other, but he had learned that it really meant where the James and Elizabeth Rivers join before flowing into the Chesapeake Bay.

*   *   *   *   *

"Well, well, well! What have we here?" said a familiar voice. The lantern was held so that Tad was blinded by the light. He could hear only a gruff voice, but he knew that it was the mean cook—the one who had threatened earlier that he wanted to get hold of the person who was feeding the cat. Tad's stomach felt sick with fear. His mouth was dry. He tried to open his lips to explain, but no words would come out.

"So yer the one who dumped the Cap'n's cream! Looks like yuh need to do some work to make up for that mess," growled the cook, as he tipped the hammock upside down. Tad felt himself spill out, banging his elbow on the deck. His funny bone hurt, and he had pain and then pins and needles all up and down his arm. "Git mov'n straight tuh the galley, bonehead," ordered the tall, hairy sailor, whose name was Shever. "Yuh got work ahead of yuh!"

Crates of bumpy brown potatoes sat at Tad's feet in the galley. Peeling potatoes was not Tad's idea of working on a ship, and seeing food caused his stomach to rumble. A pang of hunger made him realize that he hadn't eaten since morning when his mother had made hot oatmeal for him. Pa and he had walked the long muddy road to Portsmouth . . . Pa carrying the heavy tools and Tad toting the lunch of smoked ham and biscuits. They wove in and out of the cobbled streets of the town until they had come to the docks at the Gosport Navy Yard.

Now holding a dusty potato in his hand, his thoughts kept turning to the ham and biscuits, which he had left next to his father's tool box.

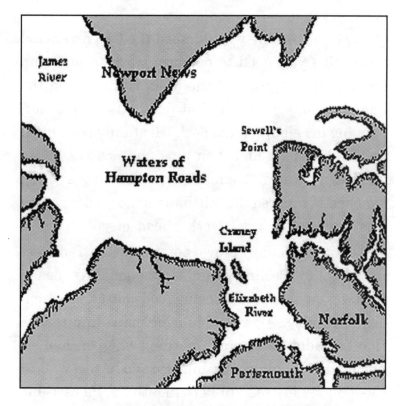

The waters of Hampton Roads, Virginia

Author's Collection

"WHAM!" The crate that Tad was sitting on shook beneath him as he saw a foot flash past. The crate rocked, almost causing him to topple.

"That's enough daydream'n. Git busy on them 'taters," ordered Shever, his greasy gray cook's hat slanted over one eyebrow. Tad's throat burned, as Shever squeezed the neck of his shirt tighter and tighter. His eyes were inches from the tattoo of a skeleton on the sailor's arm. He gasped for breath. Finally Shever let go with a yank that caused Tad to tumble off the crate. Red-faced and shaking, he climbed back onto the crate.

Tad kept peeling potatoes and tossing them into a huge pail of water. He was so hungry that he sneaked a bite of one of the potatoes.

"Cut that out!" Shever hollered. "Look, boy, if yuh like raw spuds that much, then that's what yer goin' tuh have fer dinner."

The *Virginia* was steaming slowly down the Elizabeth River, and Tad was ordered to help serve the noon meal to the hundreds of men on the ship. Shever wouldn't let him work in the officers' mess, because he didn't want Captain Buchanan to see that a young civilian boy had been left on the ship. Old Buck would be angry that he hadn't been told.

A few of the nastier men made fun of Tad. One scruffy-looking sailor, named Dagger, put out his foot causing Tad to trip. Then he forced him to get up and curtsy like a girl.

After washing, drying, and stacking the metal plates, Tad was finally given something to eat— three raw potatoes. The uncooked food made him choke and gag. After he downed two of the spuds, he ran to a pail and vomited. Shever just laughed and made him clean out the bucket and swab it with boiling water. "I thought yuh liked raw 'taters?" Shever laughed viciously.

Tad limped down the passageway to the sleeping quarters and fell exhausted into the hammock. He slept for about twenty minutes when he was awakened by a rough shaking. It was Shever.

"Git yer can out of this hammock and make yerself scarce. Cap'n's com'n this way."

Tad tumbled to the deck and quickly scurried toward the coal bunkers.

3
~~
~~

I Thought It Was a Dead Body!

"What in the name of Pete!" cried the coal hauler. "Ramsay! Ramsay! Engineer Ramsay! Come here! Quick!" called Walton.

The chief engineer hurried from the engine room to see what was causing all the commotion.

"I was just about to strike the shovel for another load when I saw a foot sticking out! At first I thought it was a dead body!" stammered Seaman Walton, still shaking with excitement. Tad could feel his face blush, although the engineers could see only a young boy blackened from head to toe from hiding in the coal bunker.

Henry Ramsay, a dark-haired officer who was sporting a large black mustache, asked, "Young man, how in the world did you get on this ship?"

13

Slowly, timidly, Tad answered in his most mannerly voice. "Sir, my name is Tad, and I came on board this morning with my father. He is one of the carpenters. I hit my head while climbing the ladder to come topside. I must have been knocked out, and the ship left the wharf before I came to." Tad was afraid to say that he had helped in the galley for fear that he might get Shever in trouble, which could give Shever a reason to punish him later.

Engineer Ramsay, who was a kindly man, gave the boy a washrag and towel. "Clean yourself up, lad, for in a few minutes we will go up to the pilothouse to meet the captain and the executive officer."

Tad hurriedly washed the coal dust from his face and hands and then followed Ramsay up the ladder. As they walked through the gundeck, several sailors who noticed their passing, stared and whistled at the fair-haired boy who had black smudges all over his hair and clothes.

Tad was nervous and his throat was dry as he climbed the ladder behind Ramsay. His hands shook as he tried to grasp each rung, and he almost got his fingers crushed by the engineer's foot as he hurried to keep up with him.

The pilothouse looked like an upside-down cone set on the forward upper deck just beyond the smokestack. Like the casemate, it was formed of wood and cast iron with walls twenty-four inches thick. There were four slits cut in the walls so that the officers could see out. In the center was a large brass wheel that was used to steer the ship.

Ramsay explained to Captain Buchanan and Lieutenant Jones how Tad had been found, and then he introduced him to the two officers. "Old Buck's" face turned red, for he was furious that a civilian boy had been left on board.

"This is the CSS *Virginia*—not a pleasure boat!" shouted the captain. Buchanan looked quite fierce. He had dark eyes, a pointed nose, and a partly balding head with wiry gray hair. Tad tensed at the captain's words. He felt as though his stomach had been turned upside down and inside out.

"Mister Jones," commanded the captain, "see me below on the gundeck . . . immediately!"

Ramsay and Tad stood at attention as the two officers went below.

* * * * *

Lieutenant Jones stood on the gundeck waiting for a scolding from his commander. He stared straight ahead. His beard and mustache were silhouetted against the brass plate which reflected the sunlight that came streaming through the grating from above. Captain Buchanan paced back

Franklin Buchanan, "Old Buck" as the sailors referred to him, was commander of the CSS *Virginia*.

and forth on the gundeck, his hands clenched behind his back.

"Mister Jones, are you aware that this is not really a trial run of the *Virginia* . . . that this is a real attack?"

"Yes, sir."

"Are you also aware of the dangers and problems that we might have with this young lad on board?" asked the captain, as he continued pacing. "There is no time to put him off the ship, you know. Who is he? And does he have a family?"

"Yes, sir," answered the lieutenant. "I understand that his name is Tad Lynch, and that he is the son of one of the carpenters who worked on the hatches this morning. Could we use him as a powder boy, Captain? I think that he's big enough to carry the powder to the guns, yet small and fast enough to scurry among the men and equipment."

"A powder boy, you say?" Buchanan thought for a moment. "I suppose so. Well, Jones, I trust your judgment and leave the matter entirely in your hands," commanded the captain. "Dismissed."

* * * * *

Peter Lynch searched frantically for Tad. No one had seen his son. Crowds of people had gathered on the wharves. Many had wished the crew luck; others had made nasty remarks about how the ship was

so big and heavy that it wouldn't float. One man
had called out, "Go on with your old metallic coffin!
She will never amount to anything else!"

Tad had been so impressed when he first saw
the vessel, that he had exclaimed wide-eyed in
amazement to his father, "Wow! You get to work on
this? This must be one of the biggest ships ever. I
wish Jimmy Allen could see me now! He's always
showing off about all the places he's been. Wait 'til
he hears about the *Virginia*! And Becky Lewis, too
. . ." Tad blushed as his voice trailed off. Mr. Lynch
knew that his son liked the neighbor girl, but Tad
seemed to want to keep it a secret.

His father explained that the *Virginia* was more
than 262 feet long, 38 feet wide, and weighed 3,200
tons. She had only a single propeller which made
it difficult for her to maneuver, so it took thirty to
forty minutes to make a turn in the opposite direction. Tad had seemed to hang on his every word.

Paul Lynch had a lump in his throat as he sadly
thought of his missing son and the possibility that
they may not have those special times together ever
again.

Now as the crowd began to disperse, Mr. Lynch
continued to question as many people as he could.
He spotted Sam Brown, one of the other carpenters
who had worked with him in the morning. He had

to weave in and out among several groups of people who were still standing at the dock discussing the strengths and weaknesses of the CSS *Virginia*. At last he got close enough to call to the older man.

"Sam, Sam! Sam Brown! Have you seen my son, Tad?" called Mr. Lynch.

"Lynch, the last time I saw your boy he was on the *Virginia*. I saw him petting a young black cat. Didn't he jump off with us when the whistle was blown?" he asked in a concerned voice.

"I thought I saw him get off, but discovered too late that it was Little John Beck who was wearing a hat just like Tad's. If you should see Tad, please tell him that he should stay here in town, go to the livery stable, and ask Cy Barker if he could stay there with him."

"Should I stay at the docks, or should I start home?" he muttered to himself. "Or should I borrow a horse and start riding along the river in hopes of stopping the ship?" He and his family would never live it down if he tried to stop the Navy in order to get his son. *And what if he isn't on the Virginia?* he thought to himself. *I'd better return home. If Tad did leave the ship, he may have headed back on the route that we took this morning. If only Star had gotten shoed, we could have ridden all the way to the docks this morning.* But there had been no money for shoeing the old horse, and there would be no money paid for today's work, because that had been volunteer labor. The Zeller family would soon be able to pay him for the table that he had built for them.

Paul Lynch left the Gosport Navy Yard and began to walk among the old cobbled streets of Portsmouth. He tried to think of what he would say to his wife. His eyes were misty as he reached the road leading out of town, passing the few small puddles that still remained from the rain that had fallen the day before. He would put the worst thoughts—that something terrible had happened to Tad—out of his mind. *Surely Tad was still on the ship. Or perhaps a family had given him a lift in their wagon and then took him home. Yes, I will find Tad safely curled up by the fire in our house.* He began to think only of good things to keep up his spirits as he trudged along the narrow muddy road.

4

~~~
~~~
~~~

What Is a Powder Monkey?

Tad followed Ramsay below, where he was introduced to the chief gunner, Charles B. Oliver.

"Oliver, I want you to show this lad all the things that a powder boy does," barked Ramsay.

"You're pull'n my leg, chief. He's too small to be a powder monkey. He looks as though the next gust of wind would blow him away."

"I am not too small! And what is a powder monkey, anyway?" asked Tad with a scowl on his face.

"Too small or not too small, that is Lieutenant Jones' order," said Ramsay, stroking his big handlebar mustache and ignoring Tad's question. "Take care of it!" ordered the chief engineer, turning on his heel.

"What is a powder monkey?" demanded Tad.

"A powder monkey is a sailor's term for a powder boy. It's the powder boy's job to carry bags of powder and other needed equipment to the gun station during battle," explained the gunner as they walked along the deck. "So, what's your name, sonny?"

"My real name is Thaddeus David Lynch, but I like to be called Tad."

Soon they came upon William Johnson, one of the gunner's mates, who was busy cleaning the forward pivot gun.

"Willy," called Oliver, "this is Tad Lynch. He's our powder boy."

"Why do we need a powder monkey?" questioned Johnson. "I thought this was just a trial run for the *Virginia*!"

"Things are a bit different now. I hear Old Buck is going to take on the entire Yankee fleet. He's going to attack the *Cumberland* first. We're going to head straight for her! It won't be long before we reach Sewell's Point, so you'll have only a short time to train the boy," pointed out Oliver. "But first, let's go below to ready the magazine hatch."

"This lad is just a little minnow!" complained the mate.

"He will do. It's Jones' order. He is your responsibility," snapped Oliver.

The CSS *Virginia*, formerly the USS *Merrimack*. Two layers of 2-inch iron plates were placed over 24 inches of wood, making the casemate 28 inches thick.

Naval Historical Center

William Norris, the master at arms, lit the lanterns in the magazine, while Smith and Johnson let down the fire screens which were large water-soaked sheets of canvas.

Then Oliver, who had gotten the keys from the lieutenant in charge, descended the ladder and unlocked the magazine that held the bags of powder as well as the different projectiles that would be fired from the guns on deck.

"Well, laddie," grumbled Johnson, "let's get started."

"This here's a pass box; it's lined with tin," explained the mate. "Inside is a wool bag that's filled with black powder. Hoist it like this and keep it upright."

Tad nodded nervously, as he shifted from one foot to the other.

"Okay. Now you try it," motioned Johnson, as he let down the pass box easily.

Tad, his legs a bit off balance, lifted the round box with his arms weaving only slightly.

"Good! We're go'in to run it to the deck now. You'll be one of the chaps who will take the powder from the forward hatch to the gundeck above, so at least you won't have to climb the ladder."

"You're small," he pointed out in a slightly gentler tone now, "so you will be good at getting in and around all the crew."

"Do I pass this thing and then come back for another one?" asked Tad.

"No, the gunner will take the bag, and you will come running back with the pass box. And then one of the mates on the ladder will place another bag of powder in it."

"Is that it?" questioned Tad.

"No, that's not all. It's a very important and dangerous job. You may also be given a shell to take to the guns. It looks like this," said Johnson, as he turned to reach for a cast iron ball. "This thing is filled with powder; it has a fuse which must be kept dry and protected. I'm just telling you in case you are ordered to carry one. Most likely you will just carry the powder bags."

"Well, I'd better get my shoes changed. It won't be long now."

"Why are you putting on different shoes?" inquired Tad.

"The gunner and the gunner's mates wear canvas shoes for safety. The canvas helps cut the chances of making any sparks. And sparks are what we do *not* need—not near all this powder! We would have the biggest fireworks ever seen—followed by an enormous fire!"

As Johnson explained some of the other safety rules, people along the banks of the Elizabeth River were waving caps and handkerchiefs to wish the crew of the *Virginia* good luck. The crowd watched in silence as the huge, lumbering ironclad, her rudder dragging slightly in the mud, pushed her way through the river channel. From her stern waved the bright red and blue flag of the Confederate States, flown proudly by her officers and crew.

Johnson reached into a bag and pulled out a gray cloth. He shook it to show a full square with two white stripes around the edge. "Put this around your neck," said Johnson. "It's a good luck scarf. You may need it!"

"Yo, down there!" called a familiar voice from above. It was Walton—the one who had discovered Tad in the pile of coal. "Chief sent me. The lad is to report to Lieutenant Jones immediately! He's on the gundeck."

"Me?" asked Tad in a small, but puzzled voice.

"You!" replied Walton, his head hanging down past the top of the ladder that led to the magazine hatch. He looked comical with the wet canvas blankets draped over his neck and only his head and stringy red hair showing, but Tad could sense that this was no laughing matter.

"Better hop to it, laddie," warned Johnson.

Tad, his face worried and his voice quavering, said, "Why does he want to see me?"

"Git!" gestured Walton, pointing his thumb backward like someone who wanted to hitch a ride on a wagon. "And don't ask questions," he commanded harshly.

Tad glanced at Johnson, who nodded in agreement, then he climbed the ladder one rung at a time, partly because he was so nervous and partly because his legs were still too short to climb the ladder one foot after the other as the sailors did. Walton had let the canvas fall, so that by the time Tad reached the next-to-the-top rung, the heavy material swatted him in the face and knocked him backward. As he began to fall, he grasped the third rung with his left hand just in time. He thought that he heard Walton chuckle.

Scurrying like a fretful squirrel, Tad scrambled aft to report to the lieutenant. He had learned that Lieutenant Jones was second in command under the captain, and he couldn't understand why such an important officer would want to see him again.

5

Please, Please . . . Let Me Stay!

His face red and still stinging, Tad found the lieutenant, ran around to his side, stood at attention, and sharply saluted. "Thaddeus Lynch reporting as ordered, sir!"

"Young man," spoke Jones in a firm, but gentle voice. "We've had second thoughts and feel that you would be safer if we put you on Craney Island. We have a few mechanics that had remained on board to help with last minute repairs. These men will be lowered in a boat and will be sent to that island where they will help the land batteries or return to their families. We intend to send you with them."

"But I want to be a powder boy," sputtered Tad, his voice choking. He tried not to whine like he

28

always did to his mother when he didn't want to do something. "Pa said that we should do all we can to help the cause . . . that our Southern states want to be independent and be ruled and governed by our own leaders. Pa helped with the carpenter work. Mother folded cloth for bandages for the wounded. Now *I* want to do something for the South!" insisted Tad.

The lieutenant listened, astonished at the youngster's strong feelings of loyalty. Then he asked with his very serious, dark eyes looking directly into Tad's, "Do you realize how dangerous this can be? This isn't a playtime with toy soldiers. This will be a full battle. There may be blood spilled. There will be sounds so loud that you won't be able to hear the man next to you, and some of the men may be shot and wounded . . . or . . . or worse yet, killed."

"Yes, sir," answered Tad in a small, but confident voice. And then in a stronger tone, "I know I can do it, sir. Please, please, let me stay. I'll be the best powder boy ever!"

Jones turned his back toward Tad and appeared to gaze out toward the federal batteries on the distant shore. Then his eyes focused on the flag fluttering from the top of the casemate, as though he were deep in thought.

Tad relaxed for a few seconds. His muscles were stiff from holding himself straight for so long. He shifted his weight so that he would not feel quite as shaky, but tensed again when he saw Jones turn to him. The officer smiled slightly. "You are the official powder boy of the CSS *Virginia*," he announced with authority. "See the quartermaster for a navy shirt. Do your duty well. Dismissed!"

Luckily Oliver had explained to him that "CSS" meant "Confederate States Ship." Just a few hours earlier Tad would not have known that bit of information, and he would have felt stupid if he had to ask a high-ranking officer what the letters meant. He snapped a salute as he had seen some of the sailors do, and smiling from ear to ear, hurried below.

The *Virginia* continued steaming north on the Elizabeth River. Off her port side—which was the left side of the ship, as Johnson had explained to Tad earlier—was Craney Island.

The ironclad's crew began to let down the thirty-foot cutter with several men in it. The boat was swaying unsteadily, and the long hemp ropes were swinging from side to side. "Steady . . . steady . . . ," called the one in charge as the cutter inched down the side of the ironclad, clanking and banging against the metal casemate. Then with a jolt and a splash, the craft smacked the water's surface, almost tossing the men into the river. They untied the lines from below, quickly pushed away from the huge vessel with an oar, and began rowing for the island.

The sailors on the gundeck pulled up the ropes and skillfully wound them into loops. Then the ropes were tied back with heavy twine. This way there was more working space which would be needed during battle.

Coming up on the starboard, or right side, of the *Virginia* were more Confederate land batteries where many men with artillery pieces were ready to fight. They had heavy cannon-like guns mounted on large wooden carriages. A few of the men saluted the *Virginia* as she passed by.

Drawing near the Confederate batteries at Sewell's Point, straight off the bow, the crew could see Fort Monroe, which the Federals had taken and occupied. And looking westward, several miles in the distance, was the town of Newport News where there were enemy land batteries. The Union soldiers were camped along the bank with their large guns pointing toward Hampton Roads.

The *Virginia* turned ever so slowly at Sewell's Point. In deeper water now, she steamed slowly westward in the North Channel. Her bow was headed toward Newport News and straight for the USS *Cumberland*.

"Pa said that people were grumbling that this ship had only one propeller. Is that true?" asked Tad.

"Yes, and that makes this ironclad really slow when she has to turn—much slower than the smaller

Chief Engineer of the CSS *Virginia*, H. Ashton Ramsay

Author's Collection

ships. She has a twenty-two-foot draft, as well," explained Ramsay.

"What's a draft?" asked Tad with a puzzled look on his face.

"That's how deep the ship needs to have the water under her in order to have room for the propeller to work at its best."

Off in the distance, the Union warship *Cumberland* swung lazily from her anchors. Her twenty-four guns were cold and quiet. It was wash day on the vessel, and the blue and white clothes of the crew were hanging from the rigging and fluttering in the sunshine. The Union tars, as sailors were often called, paid no attention to the *Virginia*. Earlier a smaller ship had seen wisps of smoke floating from the east and had signaled to the *Cumberland*, but no one had seen the signal flags. Finally, another Federal vessel fired a shot to warn the *Cumberland*.

The *Congress*, another Union ship, was closer to the *Virginia* and slightly off to the starboard side of the bow. It had forty-four guns. The sailors on the

Cumberland and the *Congress* stared in surprise as the mighty CSS *Virginia* came closer and closer. The roll of Union drums could be heard on both the land and the ships, as the crews worked fast and hard to load their guns.

Captain Buchanan, who had been directing the *Virginia* from the pilothouse at the front of the casemate, went down to the gundeck. He stood on the ladder that led to the forward hatch and turned to the crew. All heads faced forward as the men stood at attention. "Men, the eyes of your country are upon you. You are fighting for your rights, your liberties, your wives and children. You must not be content with only doing your duty, but do more than your duty!" Then he commanded the men to go to their guns. Each man returned to his station deep in thought about what the coming battle might bring.

Jones, standing beside Lieutenant Simms who was in charge of the forward gun, sent for Engineer Ramsay. The engineer climbed the ladder quickly.

"Ramsay reporting for duty, sir." As he waited for Jones to address him, he glanced past the bow and off the starboard side where he could see many sailing craft, small tugs, and boats sprinkled across the bay. He later wrote in his diary that the boats "scurried to the far shore like chickens on the approach of a hovering hawk."

Ramsay listened as Jones began speaking, explaining the signals and orders that he would most likely send when the battle would take place. "I may call you on deck later for further orders, so stay alert."

"Aye, aye, sir!" replied Ramsay, who saluted and returned below deck to await the order from the executive officer for "full speed ahead."

6

~~~

Stay Away from the Casemate!

Tad stayed on deck waiting for orders. No one had told him what to do during the lull. He looked to the bow and saw that they were closer to the enemy now. The *Cumberland* was turning slightly on her anchor so that she would soon lay across the James River Channel. As he stood on the slowly moving *Virginia*, Tad's mind turned to home.

I wonder if Pa is looking for me, he asked himself. *Mother is probably frantic. Does Jimmy Allen know that I'm missing? If only he could see me now! He would be so jealous of my being a powder boy!* he boasted silently. *And Becky . . . did she know anything about what was happening? More importantly, would she be upset? Does she know how much I like her?* His thoughts were interrupted by someone from behind.

"Well, well! If it isn't the little coal-bin beetle! How 'bout some raw 'taters, boy?" Tad recognized the voice instantly. It was Shever! He dreaded turning around to face him.

"We'll soon be ready for yuh to peel more spuds, sonny . . . not that yuh did that good of a job, anyway," scoffed the cook.

Tad just stood, his feet glued to the deck. He swallowed hard and opened his mouth, but nothing came out.

"Cat got your tongue?" taunted Shever. "Git below. Jack will give yuh someth'n useful tuh do."

Tad turned around and glared at the cook. He took a deep breath, and pretending to look as confident as he could, replied in a small but firm voice. "Lieutenant Jones has ordered me to be a powder boy for the *Virginia.*"

"What? A little runt like you! Well, if we don't beat the socks off the *Cumberland*, I'll know why," continued Shever with a sneer. "It'll be 'cause some stupid little monkey didn't get the powder tuh the guns. I don't think you'll be carry'n powder . . . you're gonna be peal'n 'taters."

If only I were bigger, thought Tad, *I would slam that big bully in the teeth.* His face reddened and he clenched his fists. Shever started down the hatch still mumbling to himself. Relief spread throughout Tad's body as Shever's head disappeared below the opening. He opened his hands to see red fingernail marks in each of his palms. His knees were still wobbly from the encounter. He looked to the bow. The *Virginia* was drawing more closely to the *Cumberland*.

Behind the *Virginia*, Confederate land batteries on Sewell's Point opened fire on three other Union warships. Because the Southern guns were firing from long range, their thunderous shots did little damage. The Union guns at Newport News were aimed directly at the *Virginia*. Suddenly, they opened fire. Their shells began to drop near the ironclad, causing huge waterspouts, much like those of a large gray whale. There were many near misses and close calls.

The officers on the USS *Cumberland* decided not to wait for the *Virginia* to strike. Fire and smoke came from the *Cumberland*'s guns. Their aim was high and the shells splashed behind the *Virginia*. The gunners on the *Cumberland* worked fast and hard to reload their guns. Now the USS *Congress* joined the *Cumberland* in trying to damage or stop the *Virginia*. Most of the shots were too wide and went to the side of the ironclad. As the *Virginia*

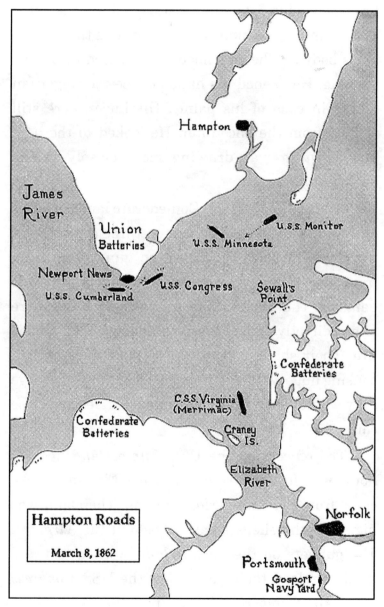

R. T. and C. R. Campbell

passed on the starboard side, the *Congress* fired a tremendous blast into the Confederate ship.

The shells crashed into the side of the *Virginia*. The force of the explosion caused Tad to lose his balance, and he fell onto the deck and slid into the hatch, hitting his arm on the top rung of the ladder. He knocked the funny bone on his elbow. It felt warm and his arm tingled all over. He pulled himself up and tried not to look embarrassed. Pieces of iron shattered against the casemate and went spinning across the water.

"Stay away from the wall of the casemate!" warned an officer, shouting over the noise. "The jolt can kill you, when the shells hit!" The whole vessel shook from the explosions. She had taken a direct hit from the *Cumberland*.

Lieutenant Charles Simms was in command of the forward pivot-rifle. He had his hand ready to pull the firing cord on the Brooke cannon that would open fire on the *Cumberland*. All that he was waiting for, was the signal from Captain Buchanan.

He got his signal, and the first shot went off with a thunderous roar. The *Virginia* shook as smoke and fire came out of her gun as the shell headed for the *Cumberland*. It streaked across the water toward the enemy ship and smashed through the starboard rail. Huge splinters went flying through

the air. Then the shell exploded. As he spun around
to return to the hatch, Tad saw some of the marines
on the *Cumberland* fall to her deck.

"Powder boy! Get this bag to the forward gun!"
One of the sailors had just run the first bag, and
now the gunners would need another.

Tad scrambled back to the hatch. Two hairy
arms holding a pass box popped up through the
hatch and past the canvas curtain. With both hands
Tad grasped the round tin with the powder bag in
it. Rounding a barrel and jumping over some thick
ropes, he raced to the forward gun. The lieutenant's
first mate took the powder bag, and Tad scurried
back to the hatch with an empty tin to retrieve
another bag of powder. His eyes watered from the
bluish smoke that was filling the casemate, and his
ears still rang from the first shot. Shells fell like
rain around the *Virginia*. Some of them bounced off
the casemate and then exploded above the gundeck,
just missing three of the gunners.

Meanwhile Simms' crew cleaned the inside of
the gun so that another bag of powder could be put
into it. Then a wad of cloth was pushed in, and
finally a 7-inch shell was rammed into the gun.

Tad returned with another bag of powder just
in time to see a crewman pull out the rammer and
put in a new primer. He had learned from Johnson

that a primer was the thing that set off a spark to fire the gun.

Simms aimed for the *Cumberland*'s forward gun. One of the men yelled, "All clear! Fire!" The blast was so loud that it hurt Tad's ears. The shell screamed toward the enemy ship. In the explosion, almost all of the crew near the bow on the *Cumberland* fell. Only the gun captain and the Union powder boy were unhurt. *I wonder what the powder boy's name is?* Tad thought. *And how old is he?*

The *Cumberland* kept firing. Her crew was amazed at how the shells just bounced off the casemate of the *Virginia*. The men pulled some of their wounded off to one side—others were carried below.

The *Cumberland* was only four hundred yards away now. The *Virginia*'s gun rattled off shells as fast as the crew could load and fire. The two were now only three hundred yards apart. The *Congress*, now on the *Virginia*'s starboard side, began sending shots into her. As the shells hit the outside of the casemate, the men inside the metal shield could barely stand the deafening noise as the sounds bounced off and echoed within the iron walls. Tad put his fingers in his ears for a few seconds to help muffle the sound.

The *Virginia* fought back hard. Lieutenant John Eggleston's men readied two guns that were filled with hot shot from the coal furnaces. Two other guns had already been loaded.

"Fire!" ordered Lieutenant Eggleston. The flaming iron solid shot crashed into the *Congress* with explosive force. One of the shots hit directly into a gun port, knocked the gun off its pivot, and killed or wounded the entire crew at that gun. Another shot hit near the magazine, setting the ship on fire. The *Congress* was crippled.

The *Cumberland* was a different matter. Nothing seemed to damage her! The *Virginia* was only a short distance from her now. The pilot of the *Cumberland* wrote in his log: "The *Virginia* looked like a huge half-submerged crocodile." She looked like a giant iron monster to the *Cumberland*'s crew.

Two friendly Southern ships, the *Raleigh* and the *Beaufort*, were trying to help the *Virginia*. They began firing at the *Congress*, so that she would fire at them instead of at the *Virginia*.

Captain Buchanan called for Chief Engineer Ramsay. Ramsay hurried from the engine room, climbed the ladder, and headed for the pilothouse. The noise was so loud on the gundeck as he passed through, that he could barely stand it.

Buchanan shouted into Ramsay's ear. "When we ram the *Cumberland*, do *not* . . . I repeat, do *not* wait for a signal to reverse the engines; just do it!" ordered Buchanan.

"Aye, aye, sir!" shouted Ramsay, nodding at the same time. He climbed down from the pilothouse, raced through the gundeck, and disappeared down the hatch to the engine room. He was ready for the ramming.

7

Fire!

"Stop the engines!" signaled the gong ringing
two times. Then the gong rang three times. "Reverse
engines!" shouted the engineer's mate. Ramsay's
hands hurriedly yanked on the levers. Silence . . .
a long pause. "Cra-a-ash!" Crewmen below deck hung
onto anything that they could get their hands on.
*Had the Virginia run aground? Was her propeller
stuck in the mud?* The great ironclad was still moving!
She was ramming the *Cumberland*! The iron prow
of the bow had smashed through the side of the
enemy craft just below the surface of the water. The
men below deck knew what the sounds of cracking
and splintering beams meant. A loud cheer sounded
from the whole crew.

Just as the *Virginia* struck, Lieutenant Simms fired his forward gun. The shell exploded deep within the *Cumberland*.

But now the prow of the *Virginia* was stuck in the side of the *Cumberland*! The *Virginia*'s engines were in reverse, working hard to back away from her. The enemy ship was sinking and pulling the *Virginia* down with her! The *Virginia* swung around still entangled with the other ship. The two vessels were almost side by side now, as they continued to fire at one another.

The CSS *Virginia* (*Merrimack*) and the USS *Cumberland*

Battles and Leaders

Tad saw that the men on the *Cumberland* had water up to their knees, but they bravely kept firing. He froze with fear as he saw that the bow of the *Virginia* was going lower and lower into the water.

With blood from the wounded men around his feet and the ironclad being pulled down, Tad wondered if he would ever see his family again. "This can't be happening!" he said. "We're sinking along with the *Cumberland!*"

Tad's mind raced. *Where do I go? What do I do?* he thought frantically. *If only Pa were here, he would know what to do.*

"Powder boy, run a bag to the stern!" shouted one of the men.

"Yes, sir!" Tad answered with a cough. He snatched the tin and bag, pushed the canvas aside, and raced for the rear of the ship where Lieutenant John Taylor Wood was manning the aft pivot gun. Lieutenant Wood's men fired shell after shell into the *Congress*, causing small fires to burst out in several places on her deck.

Tad had just gotten back to the magazine hatch when he heard Lieutenant Simms shout, "Fire!" A shell from the gun at the bow of the *Virginia* went straight for the *Cumberland*. The explosion cracked open the inner parts of the ship spraying large

Union sailors on the USS *Cumberland*. The CSS *Virginia* is in the background.

splinters of wood and long ribbons of water into the air. The Union ship rolled toward her port side then fell back, flinging her sailors across the deck. Water rushed into the gigantic hole of the *Cumberland*. There were many men lost that day.

Tad felt a sudden jerk. He grabbed onto a heavy hemp rope to keep from falling. The bow rose in the air and slammed back into the water. His feet left the deck for a few seconds, while he hung onto the rope with all his strength. The *Virginia*'s iron ram had broken off, and she was now free from the *Cumberland*. The Union ship was slipping lower and lower into the water, and her sailors were still shooting their guns in the midst of swells that came up to their waists.

The *Virginia* shot back, time and time again. Flames from the guns and explosions of shells flashed through the thick smoke that blanketed both ships.

"We've sunk the *Cumberland!* We've sunk the *Cumberland!*" shouted one of the officers.

Suddenly a crash and a burst of flame exploded just a few feet from Tad. He wheeled around and watched helplessly as a man fell to the deck.

Tad rushed below to the ship's surgeon, or doctor, who was busy tending to another man who had lost an arm when a shell had exploded. "A man down on the forward deck!" shouted Tad. Two mates followed him with a litter made of canvas stretched across two wooden poles. The two seamen worked carefully as they lifted the injured sailor onto the stretcher. They almost dumped him as they tried to fit one end of the litter through the narrow hatch. Just as the injured sailor's head disappeared through the opening, another shell exploded against the side of the casemate. It shook the deck right under Tad's feet, and sparks flew through the openings of the iron grating just above his head. One fell on his arm. He slapped at the glowing chunk with his hand. It went out quickly, burning a small hole in his sleeve and blistering his skin only slightly.

"Mew!" came a cry from under the canvas. Tad lifted the cloth to discover the cat that had gotten him into trouble in the first place. He picked up the cat just as another shell came crashing into the grating. The cat grabbed onto his shirt with its claws and buried his head under Tad's arm. Tad lifted a fire canvas, took off his neckerchief, and gently placed the animal on it. "Now you stay down there; I'll get you some milk later."

The *Cumberland* was sinking fast now. Her decks were completely covered with water. Tad could see that the sailors were rushing to get the wounded men into lifeboats. Some of the crew panicked and started jumping into the river.

* * * * *

The *Congress* was still firing at the *Virginia*. Captain Buchanan gave orders to steam up the James River, so that the *Virginia* could be turned around. Everyone knew that this was a weakness of the ship; it would take about thirty-five minutes for her to make a turn about.

As the *Virginia* started up the river, Lieutenant Wood sent three quick shots into the *Congress*, which knocked over two of the ship's guns. Then there was a lull in the firing. Things were somewhat quiet for the first time in what seemed hours to Tad. He heard the crew on the *Congress* give out a loud cheer. They thought that the *Virginia* was running from them.

Tad thought that he might have a few minutes to look for a bathroom and then maybe time to find the cat. *I'll have to think of a name for him. I know! He's as black as it is on a night with no moon . . . I'll call him "Midnight."* He rushed to the hatch where he had shoved the cat earlier to keep him out of the noise and the danger of the fighting. "Here, kitty, kitty! Here Midnight! Here, boy. Come on, Midnight."

Not seeing the cat, he looked for the ship's toilet. Johnson had told him that on a ship, one didn't say "outhouse" or "toilet," but that he should look for a door marked, "Head."

After he used the head, he went to the galley, where he searched in and among the crates for the little animal. There next to the icebox was a heap of black fur curled up on a pile of rags. "Midnight!" called Tad.

"Me-ow! Me-ow!" cried the ball of fur. Now two green eyes looked pitifully at Tad. "Me-ow, Me-ooww."

"Are you hungry, boy? Did you catch any mice for dinner?" he asked as he scratched the cat's head behind his ears. "I bet you're thirsty. Let's see if we can find some milk or cream without spilling it this time." Tad found a little dish among the crates. Then he opened the icebox, found the pitcher, and poured a small amount of cream.

"There you are, Midnight. Now stay right here and out of trouble," warned Tad. The cat lapped up the milk so fast that his tongue was just a pink blur.

Tad felt the ship come to a near stop. He almost lost his balance. When he got his sea legs again, he climbed the ladder, popped through the opening, and looked through one of the gunports to see the *Virginia* struggling to complete the turn.

"Why are we moving so slowly?" asked Tad to anyone who could hear him.

"This part of the James River is very shallow, and the propeller drags in the mud," explained one of the sailors. "She's almost turned fully now, and we're head'n straight for the *Congress.*"

8

~~~
~~~

Destroy That Ship!

"Look, three ships!" shouted a lookout.

"Thank goodness they are Confederate ships!" replied Buchanan. The friendly ships fired at the Union land batteries, keeping them so busy that they didn't have time to shoot at the *Virginia*, which was headed toward the *Congress*.

The officers on the *Congress* feared that they would be rammed like the *Cumberland*, so the crew was told to set the sails. The *Congress* was able to move about a hundred yards, but then she heaved sideways into the mud and grounded. The only working guns left on the damaged ship were the ones at the stern. The crew on the *Virginia* could see the men turning the cannons toward them.

"Old Buck says we can't get any closer to the *Congress* . . . too shallow," yelled one of the mates to another. "We're goin' after her stern!"

Captain Buchanan gave the order to fire. Within minutes the stern of the *Congress* was splintered and burning. There were other fires on the ship as well. Tad had found out that the captain's brother, Paymaster McKean Buchanan, was on the *Congress*! The brothers had split their loyalties—one went with the North, the other with the South.

It must really make the captain sad, thought Tad, *for him to have to shoot at his own brother.*

"Powder! Powder Boy!" came shouts from the gunners. Tad and two of the other mates were scurrying back and forth from the magazine hatch to the guns. One of the shells fired from the *Congress* smashed into the upper part of the casemate and slid across the top grating. Pieces of the exploding shell flew through the open squares of the metal grating, just missing Tad and piercing the arm of one of the sailors.

"A-a-h! I've been hit!" cried the man, doubling over in pain. He clutched his arm, but between each of his fingers came spurts of blood.

"Get him below to Doc Phillips!" shouted Lieutenant Wood.

The USS *Congress* on fire

The smaller Confederate ships joined in the firing, and the battle went on for about an hour. Everyone was covered with smoke and soot. Sweat was running down in streaks on their faces and necks.

Tears came to Tad's eyes when he looked through a gunport and saw men on the *Congress* falling and screaming in pain. Some of the wounded jumped overboard and drowned. He learned later that the commander of the *Congress* was killed. He quickly wiped his face on his sleeve, so that the men couldn't see him. He blinked back the tears and pretended that his eyes were watering from the smoke.

Finally, dashing among the flames, two men on the *Congress* hauled down the U.S. flag and sent up a white flag.

"A white flag! The *Congress* has surrendered! The *Congress* has surrendered!" shouted the crew on the *Virginia*.

"Cease fire!" ordered Captain Buchanan when he saw the white signal of surrender. His face looked tired, but relieved.

"Cease fire!" Lieutenant Jones shouted, repeating the command more loudly so that the rest of the crew would be sure to hear the order.

"Cease fire!" yelled a midshipman facing the opposite end of the ship. All became very quiet on the *Virginia*. Then together, all the men cheered.

Standing on top of the casemate, Buchanan shouted to Lieutenant Parker who was in charge of one of the Confederate gunboats nearby. "Parker, take the Union officers as prisoners, then remove their wounded. Allow everyone else to escape to the shore. Then make sure the ship is fully on fire."

"Aye, aye, sir," replied Parker. He ordered his men to bring the gunboat to the port side of the *Congress* to begin accepting the officers' surrender and taking care of the wounded.

Meanwhile, Lieutenant Pendergrast, now the commanding officer from the *Congress*, boarded Parker's ship. He stood at attention and saluted Parker. "Sir, as a token of surrender, I present to you my sword and the flag of the *Congress*. I ask only that you allow me to return to my ship long enough to help remove my wounded."

"I grant your request, Lieutenant," replied Parker.

Suddenly, the thunder of guns sounded again. The Union land batteries and soldiers with muskets were firing on Parker's gunboat, ignoring the white flag.

"Don't they know that we're trying to rescue their wounded men?" screamed a seaman. One of their shells landed and exploded right between two of the wounded, killing both of them. Parker blew the steam whistle to recall his men and backed away. He was able to save only twenty-three wounded Union sailors which he delivered to one of the smaller Confederate ships.

Captain Buchanan looked over at the *Congress*, which he had ordered to be burned. He was very angry when he saw just a few flames rising from her deck. "Destroy that ship!" he shouted to Jones.

Shell after shell was fired into the *Congress* until she was totally covered with flames. Buchanan was so angry with the enemy land forces for still firing, that he grabbed a rifle and climbed to the top of the ship.

"Look!" exclaimed Tad pointing upward. "The captain has a rifle!" Captain Buchanan started shooting at the enemy, when suddenly a bullet tore into his leg, knocking him painfully to the deck.

"The captain's been hit!" cried one of the mates. "Find a litter! We need to get him below to the ship's surgeon."

Two men, almost running into each other, scrambled to get a litter. One returned with the canvas stretcher, and they both climbed atop the iron shield where the captain was lying. They lifted him onto the litter as gently as they could. He winced, but bit his lip and clenched his fists to try to hide his pain from the crew. "Lieutenant Catesby Jones is in charge now," rasped the captain weakly. Tad kept just ahead of the litter bearers, moving anything that they might trip over as they maneuvered the stretcher around the guns, ropes, and down the narrow hatch.

"Doc! Doc Phillips! It's the cap'n! He's been hit in the thigh!" shouted the shorter man. Placing the litter on a table, the surgeon began to examine Buchanan's wound.

"Aren't you the powder boy?" the surgeon asked Tad. "Make yourself useful and hold this lantern so I can take a good look at this nasty wound."

"Captain, this leg will take quite a while to heal," said Phillips as he took a piece of the shattered bullet out of Buchanan's leg with a long silvery tool. He probed into another part where the flesh was torn. The captain stiffened with pain, but never uttered a sound. "And you'll have to be careful to keep it covered with clean bandages so that it doesn't get infected," warned the surgeon as he dressed the wound. When he had finished, he ordered, "You two mates take Captain Buchanan to his cabin. Make him as comfortable as possible and see that he gets some water to drink. And you," he said looking at Tad, "you lead the way with the lantern."

9

~~~
~~~
~~~

Reporting as Ordered, Sir!

The passageways below deck were narrow and dark. The same two mates carried the captain to his quarters. Tad's arm was aching from trying to hold the lantern up and away from his clothes. All of a sudden, he realized that he had not been to this part of the ship before.

"I . . . I don't know where I am or where I'm going!" blurted Tad in an embarrassed voice.

"Just keep mov'n the way yer goin', sonny. We have a way tuh go yet." The two sailors were trying to keep from scraping the bulkheads with the litter, for they knew every time that they did, the captain would feel more pain.

Finally they came to Buchanan's cabin. Tad held the door open while the men struggled to keep the stretcher from tipping as they stepped over the door sill and into the tiny room. They eased the captain onto his bunk and carefully took off his boots. "Sir!" they said, snapping a salute.

"Thank you, men. Resume your duties as before," ordered the captain.

"They forgot the water!" exclaimed Tad, after the men had disappeared. There was only silence. He tried to think of what his mother usually did when he had felt sick. "Captain, would you like the blanket on you?"

Buchanan, who looked very old to Tad, just nodded. He unfolded the gray wool blanket and spread it over the captain. "Sir, I'll be right back. I'm going to see if I can get this filled with water," he said as he took the lantern off the hook and reached for the pewter pitcher on the washstand. Then he realized that he would have to light the cabin's lamp, or the captain would be left in total darkness. He had helped his father light the lamps at home, so he knew what to do.

After the cabin's lamp was lit, Tad lifted the lantern in one hand and the pitcher in the other. He hurried along the passageways until he came to the galley. He set the lantern on a crate and reached for the handle that opened the valve on the copper water tank, while holding the container under the spout. Earlier in the day he had seen Shever get water from the tank to make coffee for the officers.

The guns above Tad were beginning to fire again. They were now shooting at the *Minnesota.* Tad worried that he was needed on the gundeck.

Trying his best to spill as little as possible, Tad threaded his way back through the passageways. "Me-ow-ow," sounded from the darkness behind him. He stopped, turned around, and held the lantern out in front of him. This only blinded his eyes with streams of light, so he tried to hold the lamp higher. It was Midnight, who began rubbing back and forth against his ankles.

"Go back, Midnight! I'm going to Captain Buchanan's cabin. You can't go there. Shoo!"

"Me-ow!" cried the cat pitifully. It seemed to be begging for attention.

The sound of the guns continued to echo through the dark passageway as Tad made his way to the captain's cabin. Voices could be heard from within. Setting the lantern on the floor, he decided to knock first.

"Come in," called a weak voice. Tad opened the door, held it with his elbow, picked up the lantern, and entered the cabin. To his surprise, there was not one man, but two, lying on the bunks. While the door was open, in jumped Midnight on quiet feet, running around to the end of the captain's bunk, but no one saw him enter. The captain cleared his throat and began speaking.

"This is Lieutenant Minor," he explained. "He was wounded in the chest by land forces when he was headed for the *Congress*. Give him water first. He's conscious, but you will probably have to hold his head and put the cup to his lips."

Tad placed the lantern on the hook. Then he picked up a cup and grasped it tightly as he poured the water from the pitcher. He put his arm under the lieutenant's head, wincing when the officer moaned in pain. He placed the cup to the man's lips and tilted it ever so slowly. The lieutenant slurped the water greedily. After several gulps he started coughing, so Tad stopped to let him rest a moment. Then he gave the officer two more sips. Next he poured a cup for the captain who needed less help and could lean on one elbow while he drank.

Lieutenant Robert D. Minor was badly wounded in the chest on the first day of the battle, March 8, 1862.

Naval Historical Center

"Sir," asked Tad, "is there anything else that you would like me to do for you?"

"Jones is commander now, but if he has a minute, I would like to talk with him. Please give him that message and let me know his response."

"Me-ow," came a call from the cat.

"What's that?" asked the captain.

"Oh! I'm sorry, sir. That's the ship's cat. I named him 'Midnight'," replied Tad quite nervously. "Sorry, sir! He followed me from the galley. I didn't know that he had gotten into your cabin. I'll get him out of here right now!"

"No, no. Forget the cat for now," said the captain. "Just get the message to Lieutenant Jones."

"Yes, sir! Right away, sir!" answered Tad with a sharp salute and a strong, loud voice, trying to cover his fearfulness. He took the lantern from the hook and left quickly, while quietly closing the cabin door behind him.

As he went up on the next deck, fewer and fewer shots were being sent from the Union land batteries, but the *Minnesota* was still returning the *Virginia's* fire. When he reached the pilothouse, Jones was looking at a chart with Lieutenant Simms. Tad, waiting to be recognized, stood at attention just outside the entrance.

Jones looked up and looking rather puzzled, said, "Yes?"

"Powder boy Lynch here, with a message from Captain Buchanan, sir!" answered Tad in a military-like manner. He tried to speak as seriously and grown-up as he could.

"Yes, what is it?" asked the lieutenant.

"The captain would like a word with you in his cabin, if possible, sir."

"Tell the captain that I will be there in just a few minutes."

"Yes, sir!" answered Tad with a brisk salute. He turned and started toward the hatch for the lower deck.

"Lynch! Come here! Help secure this magazine," barked Johnson.

"I have to deliver a message from Lieutenant Jones to Captain Buchanan," answered Tad hurriedly. "If he lets me go, I'll be right back to help."

He quickly delivered the word to the captain and was about to ask the officers if they needed him for anything else, when Jones knocked on the cabin door. As Jones entered, Tad was excused. He raced back to the magazine to help stack the bags of powder and boxes of shells.

"So you were with 'Old Buck,' were you? What did the old man have to say?" asked Johnson.

Although the sailor had taught Tad many things about being a powder boy, something told him to say as little as possible about the captain. Pa had always told him not to repeat things that someone else had said. Out of respect for the officer and his father, Tad said, "The captain is wounded and didn't have much to say. Wow! There's still a lot of powder here!" he exclaimed, changing the subject. "I'm glad all this didn't explode!"

* * * * *

While Tad worked in the magazine, Jones was sitting on the edge of Buchanan's bunk.

"I plan to stay on the *Virginia*," said the captain.

"You are really in no shape to stay on board," argued Lieutenant Jones. "We need to get you to a hospital. The sun is setting and we will soon be heading back to Craney Island."

"Lieutenant Minor, here, is the one who needs to be in the hospital; he has a serious chest wound. I'm staying!" insisted the captain. "The boy can tend to me from time to time. What is his name, again?"

"All right, if that's what you want, sir," said Jones, with a worried look. "The youngster is Tad Lynch, and I was planning on putting him off on the island with Lieutenant Minor, for he has a family and they are probably frantic by now."

"You are probably right, Jones. Perhaps we should get him off the ship while he is still safe."

* * * * *

"Have powder boy Lynch report to me," ordered Lieutenant Jones to one of the sailors as he walked by the magazine hatch.

Tad was afraid that he had done something wrong when he was told to report to the new commanding officer in the pilothouse. Tad hurried to see Jones.

"Lynch, reporting as ordered, sir."

"Lynch, you did a good job today, but for your own safety, we are going to put you off at Craney Island. We shall try to get someone to notify your family."

"But I want to stay," Tad replied disappointedly, trying not to whine. "I'll work hard. Please let me stay! May I?" he pleaded. "Isn't there some other way that you can let my father know that I'm all right and that I'm going to stay on the *Virginia*?"

"Let me think about it. If I can find someone to get a message to your parents, I'll consider it," said Jones. "You may be asked to stay with the captain, you know."

"No matter! Just so I can stay on board!" replied Tad excitedly.

10

Is He Trying to Get to Me?

Flashes from the guns had lit up the evening sky so that white clouds of smoke could be seen blanketing the *Minnesota*. Lieutenant Wood and his men had continued to fire at the enemy ship until they could barely see their target. The *Virginia* could get within only a mile of the Union vessel, for if she had tried to steam any closer, there was a chance that she might have run aground. But everyone knew that the *Minnesota* had been hit hard.

"Cease fire!" Lieutenant Jones had shouted. "It doesn't make sense to keep firing when we can't even see where the guns are pointing! We had better get out of the Roads and return to the mouth of the Elizabeth River. With the tide changing and darkness almost upon us, we might run aground," he had told Lieutenants Wood and Simms. "We've hit the *Minnesota* hard! Now let's get out of here!" The engineers and pilots were given orders to head for Craney Island. Guns still flashed from the Union land forces as the *Virginia* steamed away.

* * * * *

As the *Virginia* steamed toward Craney Island, Surgeon Phillips stopped in to check on Captain Buchanan and Lieutenant Minor. Tad moved over to the washstand to give the doctor more room.

"No, son, come closer. I need you to help dress the wounds," said Phillips.

"How do you dress a wound?" Tad asked with a puzzled look on his face.

"The dressings are the bandages," explained the doctor. "They get full of blood and need to be changed. The cloths on this tray have been washed in hot water and dried, and they are the ones that need to be placed on the wounds. Hold this tray, and I'll show you how it's done."

Tad watched the skillful hands of the doctor in awe. "Gently does it," said Phillips as he lifted the blood-soaked cloths off of Minor's chest. "You can use this pail for the old bandages." Then he carefully unfolded the brown paper that held a clean white gauze cloth. The lieutenant winced and moaned with pain as the doctor firmly placed the bandage on the open wound.

The surgeon then tended to the captain's injured leg. The dressings were stained brown with dried blood. Bright red blood was seeping around the edges. The soiled cloths were removed and fresh bandages were placed on the wound. "Keep giving them water," said Phillips. "Someone from the galley will bring chicken broth for nourishment, and Commander Jones or Lieutenant Simms will come below from time to time to check on both officers."

Soon a mate from the galley arrived with some clear soup for the men. Tad helped each of the officers sip from the metal cups. The captain was able to have some bread, but Lieutenant Minor was too weak to eat solid food.

"Get yourself something to eat now, Lynch," ordered the captain. "Go on to the galley," he motioned with his hand. Tad's face lit up. His stomach had been growling for the last hour. He scooped the cat into his arms and said, "Come on, Midnight. You and I are going to get something to eat!"

Tad wanted to avoid Shever. He was afraid that the cook would embarrass him in front of the crew or make him peel potatoes again. Shever was the officers' cook, so he went to the area where most of the sailors ate their meals. He ate the fish and corn bread hungrily, feeding a small portion of the fish to Midnight, who was rubbing his ankles and begging for food.

He started back to the captain's cabin, when a seaman met him. "Lynch?"

"Yes, I am Lynch," replied Tad with a troubled look on his face.

"A message from Lieutenant Jones: 'You have been given permission to stay on the *Virginia*, and your family will be notified by telegram when we get to Craney Island.'"

Tad smiled broadly. He was relieved that he could stay aboard the *Virginia* and happy that someone was going to let his parents know that he was safe. Johnson had taught him how to whistle, so he whistled all the way back to the captain's cabin.

* * * * *

At eight o'clock that night, the *Virginia* dropped her anchors. It had been a long day, reaping a great victory. There were two men dead and only eight wounded. Surgeon Phillips would see that the bodies were removed and that six of the wounded were taken ashore and sent to the naval hospital at Portsmouth. Captain Buchanan and Lieutenant Minor were to remain in the captain's cabin. Several other sailors were wounded on the three other Confederate ships.

It was quiet as Tad sat on a leather stool in the corner of the captain's cabin. Buchanan broke the silence. "Lynch, go find Jones and ask him if he has found out the number of casualties that the Union had today."

"Yes, sir!" Tad went down the passageway and climbed the ladder to the forward hatch just in time to see the wounded being carried off the ship by several sailors.

Tad found Jones on the gundeck and repeated Buchanan's question. After receiving Jones' answer, he hurried below and knocked on the cabin door.

The explosion of the USS *Congress*

Battles and Leaders

"Come in," called Buchanan.

"Sir," said Tad with a smart salute. "The lieutenant estimates that the Yankees lost at least three hundred men." The captain was strangely silent.

"Is . . . is that good, sir?" asked Tad timidly.

"War and death are never good," said the captain sadly, as he lay quietly in his bunk. "But, yes, the Yanks had ten times the number of killed or wounded than we did." Tad thought that he saw the captain's eyes look a bit misty. "You can go now, Lynch. Try to get some sleep," suggested the old man.

"I would not think of it, sir. Lieutenant Jones told me to stay the night with you."

"Well, then get yourself a blanket or two from my closet."

Tad opened a cabinet door and saw only piles of notebooks. He quickly closed the door and opened the one beside it. There he saw a quilt and several wool blankets. Under the quilt was a small cushion, but Tad didn't take it, for the captain hadn't offered a pillow to him. He could barely reach the shelf. His fingers grasped two of the blankets. He tugged on them until they came tumbling out, including the gray cushion. His face red and feeling embarrassed, Tad turned around to see if the captain was watching him.

"You can use the cushion," said the captain. "The seal of the Confederate Navy was sewn on it by my wife. I know that she would want you to use it."

"Thank you, sir!" replied Tad. He lowered the wick in the lamp so that the light would be dim enough to allow all three to sleep. Then he helped each of the men with a drink of water. He studied the captain's face. The deep wrinkles and the gray balding hair reminded him of his Grandfather Lynch. In deep thought about his family, he lay down on the floor with one blanket under him and the other over him. His head rested on the Navy pillow. Soon he was sound asleep.

Some of the *Virginia*'s crew stood on deck watching the *Congress* burn in the night. The sky above her was a red glow. A few of the men noticed the outline of a smaller ship pass by in the distance.

"Ka-boom!" "Boom! Crack!" Startled and frightened, Tad awoke from a deep sleep and sat up straight.

"It's the *Congress*; she's finally exploded," whispered Lieutenant Minor.

"Her crew and all of the wounded had left her earlier today. The Federals knew that she couldn't be saved," said the captain. "It's midnight, so let us try to get some more sleep." The room fell silent.

* * * * *

The next morning was Sunday, the ninth of March. Three heavy thuds awakened Tad. He jumped up and began to put on his shoes, but thought that he had better answer the door first.

A large man with a scar across his cheek was standing with a tray. "Coffee and water for the cap'n and the lieutenant," announced the mate, who stayed in the passageway. Tad carefully took the tray from the rough, hairy hands of the sailor. His upper arms had a skeleton and a knife tattooed on them. The knife had three red drops of blood dripping from the blade. Tad felt a chill run up his spine. "If yer the Lynch boy, then yer tuh come tuh the galley tuh pick up the grits and dried beef." The craggy looking man turned and left.

Shever! The cook's face was the first image to come into Tad's mind. He swallowed hard. *Is he trying to get to me, again?* His hands were shaking, and the pitcher and cups began to rattle. *If I were at home, I would be getting ready for church right now, safe with my family.* He set the tray on the washstand, hoping that the captain hadn't noticed anything unusual. He didn't want the officers to know that he was afraid of Shever, yet he knew that he had no choice but to go to the galley.

First he gave each of the officers a drink of water. Then he gave a wet cloth to the captain so that he could wash his face. He took another cloth and wiped Lieutenant Minor's face for him. Minor responded with a quiet, "Thank you."

Next Tad removed the stained bandage from the captain's thigh. He wondered if the old man would be able to walk again. Next, he unwrapped the clean bandages that Doc Phillips had left on the medicine tray. Gently, he placed it on the wound. Then he carefully wrapped a long piece of cloth around the shattered leg.

He tended to Minor's chest injury using two large bandages. The officer was much too weak to be moved. Tad awkwardly covered the bandage squares with a long strip that went under each arm and around the lieutenant's neck.

Tad put on his shoes and turned to Buchanan. "Sir, if I may be excused, I will go to the galley to get your breakfast."

"Yes, you may go, but bring Minor some broth. He is not ready for food yet."

"Yes, sir," replied Tad. He picked up the tray and hurried straight to the head, for he felt as though he were ready to burst. Anyway, it would postpone the misery of going to the galley for just a few more minutes.

11

What Is Going on Here?

The lanterns that hung in the passageway gave barely enough light to see. As he neared the galley, Tad could hear the clanking of pots and pans along with swear words and yelling by the sailors as they went about cooking and dishing out food. Tad slowly poked his head around the corner, hoping not to be spotted until he could see who was there. Sure enough . . . there was Shever. Tad decided to wait a few minutes. Shever turned around and began unpacking a barrel.

Now's my chance, thought Tad. He scurried into the galley and stood before one of the mates. He wanted to avoid saying his own name, for fear that Shever would look up. "I'm here for the captain's

76

breakfast," he announced, trying not to speak too loudly.

"Yo, Shever!" a portly sailor called. "Did someone set aside the cap'n's grub?"

"Yeah," said Shever as he turned toward the men. It's right h . . . Well, well, if it isn't our little powder monkey!" he scoffed. "Logan, give the pest the food that's on that metal plate . . . the one with the lid." Then he winked and nodded his head at the mate with the skeleton tattoo, who then exited to the passageway.

Logan loaded a tray with the food and utensils and handed it to Tad. Afraid that he might say the wrong thing, Tad said nothing. He turned, rounded the corner to the passageway, and held the heavy tray against his waist to keep his balance. This part of the ship was almost dark. He slowly walked several more steps, waiting for his eyes to adjust, when he felt his ankle catch on something. His whole body went forward, and he felt himself falling. He grasped the tray, trying not to upset the food and plates. He came down hard onto the deck. His head crashed into the tray—which he managed to keep clutched tightly in his hands—but everything else went flying. As he lay sprawled on the deck in the darkened passageway, he heard footsteps running back toward the galley.

He got to his knees, then up on his feet. Leaning against the bulkhead for support, he felt something warm run from his nose to his lip. He touched his upper lip. Blood was on his fingers. With his head hurting and his nose bleeding, he tried to think about what to do next. *Do I return to the galley for another tray of food? Should I report back to Captain Buchanan? Should I let anyone know that I was tripped . . . or will no one believe me and think that I was just clumsy?*

"Lynch! What is going on here?" It was Johnson.

"S . . . Someone tripped me. I was taking a tray to the captain. Whoever it was, ran back to the galley. Now I . . . don't know . . . what to do," Tad said in an embarrassed, sobbing voice.

"Here. Use this to wipe your face," Johnson said as he picked up the napkin that lay near the tray.

"But that's . . . that's the captain's napkin!" whined Tad.

"Just do it!" commanded the sailor. "I'll help you pick up this mess, then we're going back to the galley."

Tad shuddered to think that he had to deal with Shever again. He wiped his face and stooped to help gather the metal plate and utensils. He put the clumps of food on the tray and wiped the deck as well as he could.

"Let's go!" ordered Johnson.

With his heart pounding, Tad plodded along behind Johnson, dreading to have to face Shever. He had no idea what to say to him.

Just before they reached the galley, Johnson pushed Tad ahead of him. "Go on."

"Well looky here! Shever called, spotting Tad with the messy tray. Did you trip over your own feet, you clumsy monkey?"

Before he could answer, Johnson spoke. "What makes you think that the boy tripped? How do you know that he didn't accidentally run into someone?"

"I . . . uh, jest guessed," Shever stammered, his face turning red.

"Get Lynch a clean tray with hot food and a cup of coffee . . . quick! A clean napkin is needed as well."

Shever snatched a linen cloth from the shelf where the officers' napkins were stored and flipped it onto the tray. Next, he slammed down another plate of hot food.

"Is that all, your Royal Prince of Pests?" said Shever belligerently, as he looked at Tad.

"Broth in a cup and a napkin is needed for Lieutenant Minor," replied Tad, facing Johnson. He avoided looking at Shever.

"Next you'll be wanting flowers!" snarled Shever, cursing under his breath. Then he turned his back to them, still mumbling to himself. He poured the broth and got another napkin. He started to hand the tray to Johnson.

"Not to me, stooge . . . give it to Lynch! And put some bread and sausage on there for the boy."

Shever begrudgingly added more food and handed the tray to Tad.

Johnson motioned for the boy to leave. Tad silently mouthed a "Thank you" to him, then turned to go. *And thank you, Lord,* Tad murmured to himself, looking up, as he often saw his mother do.

* * * * *

While the captain was drinking his coffee, Tad helped the lieutenant with his cup of broth. Then he hungrily ate his own meal. Just as he was finishing, a loud knock sounded on the cabin door.

"Enter!" ordered the captain. It was Lieutenant Jones.

"Good morning, sir," said Jones as he saluted. "Surgeon Phillips feels that you and Lieutenant Minor should be taken off the ship here at Craney Island. Then both of you can be taken to a hospital in Norfolk to receive better care."

Just then the doctor entered the cabin. "Good morning, Captain." And looking over to Minor and nodding, "Lieutenant. I feel strongly, sir, that both of you need to get to a hospital as soon as possible," said Phillips.

"No, I plan to stay on board!" insisted Buchanan.

"But, sir, you must reconsider! Not only is it important for you to get better medical care, but this space may be needed for the men who may be wounded when we begin fighting again," pleaded the doctor.

Buchanan thought for a moment. "Perhaps you are right," he said. "I'm no good to the men in this condition. And Minor definitely needs more care."

"Yes," replied Phillips, "the lieutenant has a fever."

I will make the necessary arrangements," said Jones. "Is there anything else, sir?"

"No. Just keep up the good work. I have the utmost confidence in you."

"Thank you, Sir. I will send for the two of you shortly. Good day," he said as he saluted.

As the doctor was leaving, he looked at Tad and smiled. "Lynch, you did a fine job with those bandages."

"Thank you, sir." Tad's eyes remained downward.

"Sir," Phillips said as he saluted the captain. "I will see you on deck."

Tad pretended to study the design in the quilt. His eyes were filling with tears, for he had grown quite fond of Captain Buchanan. One minute he wanted to leave the ship in order to stay with the captain, but the next minute he wanted to remain aboard the *Virginia* to carry out his duties.

"You have been a dependable powder boy on this great ship, Master Lynch," said the captain. "I have heard that some of the men give you a hard time. I know more about what goes on than you think I do. You must hold your head high, for you have served the CSS *Virginia* and its crew well. I am sure that you will want to continue serving as a powder boy. The next action is the attack on the USS *Minnesota*. I wish you luck, lad."

"Thank you, sir." It was settled. Tad knew that he was expected to fulfill his duty as a Confederate sailor. He would not let the captain down.

＊ ＊ ＊ ＊ ＊

After the crew finished eating their breakfast, they began to get the great ironclad ready for departure. Three other smaller ships—the *Patrick Henry*, the *Jamestown*, and the *Teaser*—would sail along with the *Virginia*.

The coal heavers began to shovel coal into the huge furnaces. The pumps for steam pressure were started, and the men oiled the many parts of the machinery so that the *Virginia* could steam back to the waters of Hampton Roads. The crews of

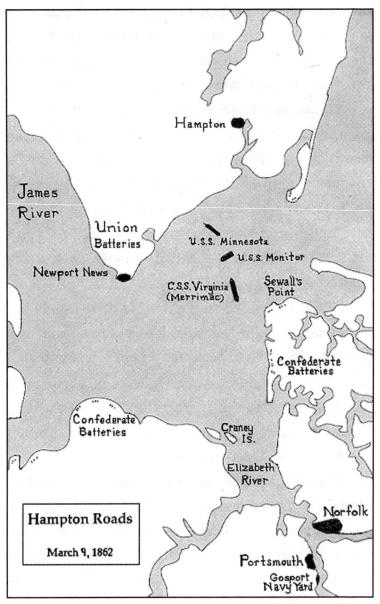

Hampton

James
River

Union
Batteries

U.S.S. Minnesota

U.S.S. Monitor

Newport News

C.S.S.Virginia
(Merrimac)

Sewall's
Point

Confederate
Batteries

Confederate
Batteries

Craney
Is.

Elizabeth
River

Norfolk

Hampton Roads

March 9, 1862

Portsmouth

Gosport
Navy Yard

R. T. and C. R. Campbell

Lieutenant Simms and Lieutenant Wood worked to clean and oil the pivot guns. Others worked on the side guns. There was no time to repair the two gun barrels that were broken.

The sailors went to their stations where each man had a job to do. Some of the men stood in the passageways where their job was to pass the shells and powder up to the gundeck. Tad was ready to carry the powder bags to the gunners.

"Lynch, come over here and hold this pole so I can tie our flag to it," called a mate with a big mustache.

"What happened to the flag?" asked Tad as the sailor handed him the pole. He could see that the pole was old and had been tied where it was cracked.

"It got shot down when we were at battle with the *Congress* yesterday." After they secured the flag, Tad helped the sailor shove the long pole up through the grating of the casemate.

The anchor was raised just after sunrise. The gong rang in the engine room, and Engineer Ramsay pulled the levers and started the engines. Slowly the iron craft moved toward Hampton Roads, seeking the enemy. The Confederate flag waved brilliantly in the early morning sun.

The *Minnesota* was four miles away and still stuck in the muddy waters of the Roads. Jones stood on the iron grating of the top deck and looked through his marine glass. He saw a strange-looking ship near the *Minnesota*. The *Virginia* had to be stopped when they got within a mile, for there was danger that her rudder might drag on the bottom of the Roads again.

Tad had carried a bag of powder to the forward gun, and Lieutenant Simms gave orders to ready the gun for firing. Just then the odd-looking vessel started toward the *Virginia*.

12

There Is a Leak in the Bow!

The strange ship coming toward them had a large round turret on top. And now she was heading straight for the *Virginia*. Tad had hauled two more bags of powder to the bow. When he brought the third, he saw Simms getting ready to pull the lanyard to fire a shot. The Union ship was the mighty *Monitor*. Suddenly her turret turned, and out of it blasted two shots with smoke and flames.

The shells crashed and exploded onto the casemate of the *Virginia* so hard that it cracked some of the iron plates. The noise was so loud that Tad and most of the men covered their ears. The terrible sound echoed over and over again. One of the shells exploded when it hit; the other bounced off the iron casemate and fell hissing into the water.

The two ships headed for one another. For two hours, the *Monitor* and the *Virginia* fought ferociously. They even began to circle one another. The *Virginia* was very slow at turning. The *Monitor* was much faster. The *Virginia*, though, could fire up to five of her guns all at one time. The *Monitor* had only two guns within a revolving turret.

"Powder!" shouted one of Simms' men, again. Commands from the officers could barely be heard among the crashing shots from the enemy and the firing from the *Virginia*'s guns. Tad hurriedly made his way through the smoke, almost running into

Lieutenant Catesby R. Jones, executive officer of the CSS *Virginia*

Naval Historical Center

Shorty, who was on his way back to the hatch from delivering powder. Shorty had been given the job of powder monkey, because he was a very small man, less than five feet tall. Today, it was Tad's and Shorty's job to run powder to the pivot gun at the bow of the ship. Others ran powder to the aft, starboard, and port guns.

The gun crews on the *Virginia* were loading and firing as fast as they could. Every time the guns were fired, flames leaped from the muzzles, causing the gun crews to jump aside so that they would not be burned. Shells merely bounced off the eight-inch-thick iron gun turret of the *Monitor*. The *Virginia* had met her match.

The noise was unbearable as the *Monitor* rapidly returned fire into the *Virginia*. The whole ship shook as shells slammed against her casemate.

Tad was startled by a shout. "It's Shorty! He's been burned!" yelled one of the gunners. Shorty had gotten too close to one of the flaming guns. Some of the loose powder had exploded as well. The left side of his face, shoulders, arms, and hands were black. He staggered under the shock. One of the other men laid him down on the deck and shouted for a litter. By this time, the wounded sailor was shrieking in pain. The litter bearers lifted him onto the stretcher and carried him through the hatch and down the ladder to Surgeon Phillips.

Tad, the gunners, and most of the others on the gundeck were blackened from the smoke. Each worked as hard and as fast as they could to carry powder, ready the guns, and fire shells at the *Monitor*.

Suddenly the *Virginia* shook . . . then lurched forward and then back. She had gone aground! Her thrashing propeller was churning in mud.

The *Monitor* circled and fired upon the *Virginia* with no mercy. Shell after shell exploded against the iron casemate. The ship trembled and shook each time her casemate took a battering. The Federals now had the advantage.

"Lynch, run to the engine room!" ordered Lieutenant Jones. "Tell Engineer Ramsay to try cotton and anything he can get his hands on to make the furnaces burn hotter! We need to get more power from those engines!"

Tad obeyed immediately, running as fast as he could. Before he could reach the hatch, a shot skimmed across the top of the casemate and exploded with a thunderous jolt. Pieces of fiery metal came flying through the openings of the grating just above Tad. Blistering hot fragments hit his arms and his legs. His thick shirt saved him. He was not so fortunate with his leg. A piece of smoldering metal pierced his stocking just below his pant leg, bit his flesh, and passed on, grazing him just above his ankle. He limped in pain as he went down the ladder.

He found Ramsay and his men working in the sweltering hot engine room. They were desperately trying to find a way to get the propeller to turn faster. The coal haulers and heavers threw on more coal. Next, the crew piled on oiled cotton and splints of wood—anything to keep the furnaces burning as hot as possible to force the engines to work harder and faster. The propeller was grinding, and churning, and squealing. Finally the ironclad slowly dragged herself free. The whole crew cheered.

Shells from the *Monitor* continued to batter the *Virginia*'s casemate as she slowly turned. The *Virginia*'s crew returned fire, but nothing seemed to penetrate the iron monster. Lieutenant Jones came down from the spar deck. He looked over at one of the gun stations, where not one man was working. The men were just standing there!

"Why are you not firing, Mr. Eggleston?" demanded the commander, trying to be heard among the loud noises from the casemate.

"It's a waste of ammunition, sir," yelled the lieutenant. "We have not been able to damage the *Monitor* . . . not even a trifle."

"Keep shooting!" ordered Jones. "We are getting ready to ram her!"

After nearly an hour of trying to turn to a position where they could ram the enemy ship, the *Virginia* was ready at last. Jones had ordered Ramsay to reverse the engines at the very second they struck the *Monitor*. This way they could back away from the *Monitor* without doing any damage to themselves . . . hopefully.

"All ahead full!" ordered Jones. The gong in the engine room rang. The *Virginia* began to gain speed.

At the last minute, the *Monitor* turned and the *Virginia* merely glanced off the side of her bow.

"I don't think we caused any damage to her, sir," said Simms disappointedly.

One of the mates ran to Simms and Jones, giving a quick salute. "Sir, it has been reported by the ship's carpenter that there is a leak in the bow!" the sailor announced, shouting over the clamor.

Just then a loud boom sounded. Both of the *Monitor*'s guns were pointing at the *Virginia*. An eleven-inch-wide shell crashed against the casemate. The force of the explosion rocked the whole ship, causing Wood's men at the aft gun to fall painfully to the deck. The noise was so loud that some of the

The USS *Monitor* and the CSS *Virginia* fought for more than three hours. Neither could gain an advantage over the other.

Battles and Leaders

CHAPTER TWELVE

Lieutenant John Taylor Wood who commanded the aft gun on the CSS *Virginia*

Library of Congress

men were bleeding from the ears and nose. One of the men hit his head on the rail under the casemate.

Tad ran to help the unconscious sailor. His face was down against the deck.

"It's Shever!" yelled another mate. Tad hesitated for a minute, then grabbed some of the empty powder bags. Kneeling, he carefully put the cloth under the cook's head and called for a litter. Two men carefully lifted the limp body, while Tad placed the bags on the stretcher so that Shever would have something soft under his head. He was taken below deck to Doc Phillips.

Jones ordered his crew to bring more powder to the gun stations and to reload all the guns. Johnson stood on the ladder at the opening of the hatch with his strong arms holding the tin pass box of powder. Tad, blackened with smoke, hurried to the bow of the ship with the powder. Others ran powder to the side guns.

Both the *Monitor* and the *Minnesota* fired at the *Virginia*. One of the times when the two Union ships parted, the *Virginia* fired a shell into the *Minnesota* that passed through several sections of the ship and exploded, ripping four rooms to shreds.

"The leak in the bow is not serious as long as the bilge pumps are kept running," reported Ramsay. "The casemate has been pushed in about three inches, but if we're not hit in the very same spot, she should hold."

As the Union ship rounded the stern of the *Virginia*, Lieutenant Wood and his men aimed their cannon at the enemy vessel. The gun fired. The shell struck the pilothouse of the *Monitor* and exploded. Pieces of molten iron sailed through the viewing slits, injuring the Union commander. It was reported later that he had been badly burned and blinded, but that after the battle he could see again.

The *Monitor* was quiet now. She turned her bow away from the *Virginia* as fast as she could. As the men on the *Monitor* tended to the injured leader, their ship was steaming away from the *Virginia*.

"Her crew is probably hauling more supplies and ammunition from below decks," said Simms.

"No, the *Monitor* has turned and fled," said Jones. "Head for the *Minnesota*!"

"We cannot remain in the Roads," argued one of the pilots, "for the river tide will cause these waters to become even more shallow than they already are. We shall surely run aground if we stay!"

Jones talked it over with his lieutenants. It was decided that, for now, the *Virginia* would head for the Elizabeth River and return to Norfolk for repairs.

When the *Virginia* was seen steaming south, the new commander of the *Monitor* thought that the *Virginia* had given up the fight.

The crew on each ship thought that the other one had withdrawn from battle! Both cheered and shouted, "Victory!"

13

I Know His Eyes Will Pop

"Wow! Look at all the people!" exclaimed Tad as he climbed on top of the iron casemate. The Confederate banner waved in the bright sunlight on this Sunday afternoon of March 9. Crowds stood along the banks and wharves of the Elizabeth River waving flags and cheering as the huge craft steamed past. Four other smaller ships ran along the port and starboard sides of the great ironclad. The breeze ruffled Tad's hair as he held his head high. He waved to the men, women, and children who had gathered to honor the now famous CSS *Virginia* and her gallant crew.

Just then he felt a hand on his shoulder. "Hey, there," said a voice. Tad whipped around. He flinched and swallowed hard when he saw that it was Shever.

"Just wanted to thank yuh for help'n me when I was down," the cook said in a serious voice. "I heard that I was out cold and that yuh held muh head and fixed a pilla outa powder bags fer me. That right?"

"Yes," answered Tad meekly. "Are you all right, now? Do you know how Shorty is?"

"Yeah, I'm okay. Shorty's fine, too . . . jest slightly scorched . . . no big burns or noth'n. I want yuh to have muh lucky halfpenny," offered Shever holding out his hand. "Not jest fer help'n me, but fer be'n a great powder monkey. And, here's muh neckerchief, too. It has the Confederate Navy emblem on it."

"Thank you," replied Tad, accepting the coin and the cloth. He was astonished that the usually mean sailor could speak so kindly. Shever gave the boy a salute, turned, and disappeared into the crowd of men. It was the first time anyone had ever given him a salute. He felt like a real sailor now.

They were almost to Norfolk and just beyond that, was the Gosport Navy Yard at Portsmouth. Soon he would be home. That, too, was a good feeling. He couldn't wait to tell Jimmy Allen about all his adventures.

Wait 'til I see Jimmy, thought Tad smiling. *I know his eyes will pop out when he sees my souvenirs—proof that I . . . Thaddeus David Lynch . . . really was on . . .* "the great, the famous CSS

Virginia!" he shouted into the wind. *And Becky,* he thought, *I hope that she has missed me.*

At last the *Virginia* arrived at the navy yard. She was skillfully maneuvered into the slip at the dock. The engines were completely shut down and her anchors were dropped. Then she had to be tied securely. Finally the gong sounded for those of the crew who had permission to leave the ship.

Tad had mixed feelings. He wanted to stay on the *Virginia*. He was proud that he had helped the South and proud to have served in the Confederate States Navy. Yet, at the same moment he was really happy to be going home. Now every person in his family had worked to help the cause in one way or another.

As he stood with the crowd of men waiting to disembark, he wondered if he could hitch a ride from Portsmouth to his house. If not, he would walk home. He'd certainly done it before . . . just never alone. As he walked down the gangway, he heard someone shouting, "Tad! Tad!" His head bobbed from side to side trying to look around the sailors who were standing in front of him.

"Tad! Here! Over here!" He recognized the voice. It was his father's. First he saw Pa's hat and then his smiling face. He ran into his father's arms. Pa's big bear hugs always felt wonderful. Then Tad re-alized that some of the crewmen might be watching him, so he straightened up and shook his father's hand, trying to look like a grown-up.

"Pa, I thought that you might be angry with me! Are you? Where's Mother? How's Scamp?"

"Whoa! Not so fast! Too many questions at once. Mother is fine and can't wait to see you. She's making a special dinner for your homecoming. Scamp misses you, too. He ran into your room this morning and came out whining. And, no, I am not angry with you. I was at first, but when we received the message, we were relieved that you were alive. When we found out that there was a real battle on the *Virginia*, we were more afraid for you than angry. Your mother and I are just glad that you have returned safely. You must have some interesting stories to tell us."

"I sure do!" said Tad excitedly. "Wait until you see what I brought back with me. Are we walking?"

"No," answered Pa. "Star is hitched up to the wagon."

The two walked to the hitching post near Walker's General Store. There was Star waiting patiently.

"Star will need water before we start for home," said Pa, reaching for the wooden pail from the back of the open wagon.

"Let me give it to her," Tad called out eagerly. He loved Star almost as much as Scamp. He patted her nose gently, and Star gave a friendly whinny. They walked over to Barker's livery stable and filled the pail with water. Pa helped Tad carry the heavy bucket. Star lapped the water thirstily.

* * * * *

"Whoa!" Pa called to Star, but the mare had already slowed her pace when she approached the cabin. She knew to stop, for she had traveled the route many times.

Mother ran out of the front door the minute she heard the wagon. "How's my big sailor?" she asked. Tad climbed down from the wagon seat and stood as tall as he could to impress his mother. A barking sound came from the direction of the tool shed. With his tail wagging and ears flopping, Scamp raced toward Tad. "You might think that Scamp had not seen you for a month!" exclaimed Pa. Tad knelt on the ground and held out his arms for his beloved pet. The dog jumped at his master so hard that he knocked him over onto his back. "Scamp! Did you miss me, old boy?" The dog licked Tad's face with his large sloppy tongue. "I missed you, too!" said Tad laughing.

"Now wash up for supper at the pump, you two," ordered Mother. "The meal is ready, Tad, and we are having your favorites—chicken with dumplings and apple cobbler for dessert."

14
Who Sent Him?

"You just made up that stuff about the mean cook," scoffed Jimmy Allen. "And anyway, he would not have been nice to you later."

"Tad does not lie!" argued Becky. Tad's face lit up when Becky took his side.

Jimmy still looked doubtful. Tad showed the neckerchief and the halfpenny to them and explained who Shever was and why he had given the gifts to Tad. Then he showed them the small wound that was healing on his ankle.

"Wow!" exclaimed Becky. "A hero . . . that is what you are . . . a real hero!" Tad blushed. "May I try on the neckerchief?" she asked.

"And may I see the coin?" asked Jimmy. Tad hesitated. "Please?" begged Jimmy.

"Oh, all-l-l right," answered Tad, trying not to sound like a showoff. But he glowed inside.

* * * * *

Tad hurried across the field and along the path. The last quarter mile of his walk from school always seemed the longest. Perhaps it was because Becky and Jimmy reached their houses first. They were lucky to live closer to the schoolhouse than he. Becky's house was closest to school. A few hundred yards from Becky's was Jimmy's house. Tad liked it when Jimmy was absent—which wasn't very often—because then he could walk all the way home with just Becky. He could tell her things that he would never say in front of Jimmy.

Here the path widened to make room for the large oak tree where he often played. Then came the shadowy hollow just before the small hill. As Tad hiked over the ridge, he saw a horse and carriage in front of his house. He could not make out who was standing there. As he drew closer, he squinted and could see two men. One was in the driver's seat. The other, who was standing beside the horse, appeared to be wearing a naval officer's uniform.

Scamp leaped through the grassy field, barking and dancing. He was so excited to see his master. Tad ran to meet him. "Hey there, Scamp. Did you miss me while I was at school? Let's see who the visitor is. Come on!" The two raced, but Scamp always won. Just as Tad got to the water pump, his mother opened the door to greet the strangers.

"Hello!" called Tad to the visitors, as he tried to catch his breath.

"May I help you?" asked Mother as she faced the guests.

"Is this the residence of Master Tad Lynch?" inquired the officer.

"Yes. That is my son, who is standing behind you. And I am Mrs. Lynch, Tad's mother."

"How do you do, Ma'am. I am Lieutenant King. I have a package and a message for you, Master Tad. This box must be opened right away," he said pointing to the carton on the seat of the carriage. He lifted the box carefully and gently set it on the ground.

Tad could not imagine what it could be. "Is it really for me?"

"Yes, it is," said the officer. "You should open it."

Tad tossed his books on the grass and eagerly walked over to the surprise. "Master Tad Lynch," was written on the top in large block letters. The box had several holes punched in it. He lifted one of the flaps. "Midnight!" shouted Tad, awakening the cat, who blinked in the bright sunlight. "I thought that I would never see you again! Mother, look! This is the cat that I told you about! Who sent him?"

asked Tad looking first at his mother and then to
the bearer of the gift.

"Me-ow!" cried Midnight. Tad scratched the cat's
head, just behind his ears. "Me-ow," cried Midnight
again, as he rubbed his head against Tad's hand.

"You said that there is a message?" asked Mrs.
Lynch, turning to Lieutenant King.

"It is sealed," said King. He handed the letter
to her. Seeing that it was addressed to Tad, she
promptly gave it to her son.

"Wow! This wax seal is the fancy kind," Tad
exclaimed as he examined the paper. I saw this
same emblem on a pillow when I was on the *Virginia*. And it's the same one that's on Shever's
neckerchief! It's the Confederate Navy seal!" he
cried out in excitement.

"If you will excuse me, I must be going," announced the lieutenant. "I am due back at the navy
yard in less than an hour."

"Certainly." "Would you like some lemonade or
tea before you start back?" Mrs. Lynch asked politely.

"Thank you, just the same, Ma'am. I have a
canteen, and I really must be on my way. Good day,
now."

"Good-bye, and thank you," said Tad.

Tad carefully pulled the flap of the letter until
the gray wax cracked and the paper was loosened.

He unfolded the important looking document, and curiously studied it. "It's from Captain Buchanan!" cried Tad, as a big smile spread across his face.

"Go ahead and read it!" prompted Mother.

Just then Mr. Lynch came up the lane riding Star. "Pa! Pa!" shouted Tad, waving the letter.

Pa slid off the saddle and onto the ground. "Who were those men? And what is all the excitement?"

"Look what Captain Buchanan sent to me! Midnight!—the cat from the *Virginia* that I was telling you about!"

"There's more," said Mother. "The captain also sent this beautiful letter," she said, pointing to the delicate rice paper.

"There is one word that I'm not sure how to pronounce," said Tad. He handed the paper to his mother who read the fancy lettering aloud.

For: **Thaddeus D. Lynch**, *Powder Boy*
who dutifully and courageously
served his country,
the Confederate States of America,
on the **CSS Virginia**
March 8 and 9, 1862.
Signed: **Franklin Buchanan**, *Captain*
CONFEDERATE STATES OF AMERICA
Navy Department, March 12, 1862

When Mother finished reading the document, all three of them were beaming. "Congratulations, Tad," she said.

"You deserve it, sailor," said Pa, shaking his son's hand.

"Thank you," said Tad proudly, as he nodded his head and took a low, gentlemanly bow, as though he were a performer on a stage.

"Perhaps Pa will make a frame for the letter," suggested Mother. "It should be kept clean and dry. You can even show it to your children some day."

But Tad wasn't listening. He was hugging the cat. "Isn't Midnight terrific?" he asked, not waiting for an answer. "I told you that he was a pretty cat. At first the sailors said that he was bad luck, because he was all black. But then I showed them this little white spot on his belly," he said as he pointed to the milky patch of fur. "That little bit of white saved his life and made it so that the crew let him stay on the ship. Let's go get some milk for you, little one."

"Woof! Woof!" barked Scamp.

Tad gave the dog a pat. "I love you, too, Scamp. This is Midnight," he explained as he let Scamp sniff the newcomer. The cat's hair stood straight up as he arched his back and hissed at the yellow dog. Scamp backed up, then, again, cautiously went to the cat. He gingerly licked Midnight, as though he were thinking, *We can be friends*.

At supper that night, Tad told even more stories than he had the evening before. "And guess what else happened one night when Midnight was in Captain Buchanan's cabin?" He talked all during the meal. Midnight drank some milk and licked himself clean. Then he walked over to his box in the corner of the pantry where he fell asleep on an old piece of soft flannel. Scamp's ears stood straight up. He creeped across the floor a little at a time until he finally reached the box. Scamp licked Midnight's fur and lay down guarding his new friend.

15

Virginia

"Here kitty, kitty, kitty!" called Tad. He opened the door of the shed. For the past few days, Midnight had begun to hide in Mr. Lynch's workshop. Tad began searching and found him behind a pile of lumber. Straddling a small stack of chair rungs, Tad peered over the bulk of the wood. "Wow! I'll be a monkey's uncle!" he whispered. There was Midnight lying on some rags with baby kittens at her side. "One, two, three, four, five, six!" counted Tad. "Six furry kittens!"

"Mother! Pa! Come quickly!" Tad shouted running toward the house.

"Is something wrong?" called Mrs. Lynch with a worried look on her face. "What is it?" asked Pa who had just come in from feeding Star.

"It's Midnight" he said, catching his breath. "He's a she!"

"What on earth are you talking about?" asked Mother.

"Midnight had six babies! He, or rather *she,* is in the shed. I found all of them behind the big pile of lumber," exclaimed Tad.

Several weeks later, the Lynches discovered that there were five male kittens and one female kitten. Tad had changed their names several times. He began renaming the male kittens. "Let me see, one can be 'Shorty,' because he is the smallest one. The second kitten will be 'Buck,' because he is a leader. This one is 'Shever,' being mean sometimes and well-behaved at other times. This one is 'Ramsay,' who is gentle and smart. That one is 'Johnny,' named for Johnson, who trained me to be a powder boy on the *Virginia.* 'Virginia!' Yes! That will be your name, little girl! You are gray and strong," he said, petting the only female in the litter! "After all, I found your mother on the CSS *Virginia,* so that is what your name will be—Virginia!"